Some comments on **Purpaleanie and other Permutations:**

"A good storyteller is worth the salt in his soup. He is worth the whole pot, complete with chunks of tender red meat. And then some. Everyone loves a good storyteller.

"Stan Wiersma, who writes under the penname of Sietze Buning, is such a storyteller. Not only does he tell stories simply and beautifully but he interprets them."

— Harold Aardema, The Doon (Iowa) **Press**

"I like Purpaleanie and other Permutations *very much indeed . . . . I like all them in their different ways. They have created a new world of childhood for me: touching, funny, and in a universe, a sort of post-Eden Eden."*

— Christopher Fry

"Sietze's lyrics capture the mood and temper of characters and conflicts too real, too homely, too rich to lose negligently. There's more heritage in one night's huisbezoek *with Sietze Buning than in a lifetime of Tulip Fests."*

— James C. Schaap, Dordt College

On "Last Visit in Three Voices":

" . . . there are lovely tones of voices here, and rituals, and ways of doing things that are usefully common to us all."

— Robert Creeley

On "Afternoon with Eliot":

" . . .wry intelligence and tasteful reverence."

— Judson Jerome

Purpaleanie
and other Permutations

Sietze Buning

photographic permutations by Carl Vandermeulen

The Middleburg Press • Orange City, Iowa • 1978

The publisher wishes to thank
Hugh Cook
and
James Vanden Bosch
for helping the Middleburg Press
produce its first book.

Library of Congress
Catalog Card Number 78-61207

ISBN: 0-931940-00-1

Printed and bound
in the United States of America

Book and cover design
by Carl Vandermeulen

Some photos bear comment:
All have undergone permutation through
a photographic process called solarization.
The cover and title page photos
are of Middleburg, Iowa.
The illustration on page 91 shows the old
Middleburg Christian Reformed Church.
The photo for page 73
was taken from the Orange City **Centennial Book**

Voor twee vaderen Israels

JAN TIMMERMAN

en

WILLEM SPOELHOF

Zoals de cederbomen
hoog op de Libanon,
staan bij de levensbron
de nederige vromen.
Die in Gods huis geplant zijn,
zij bloeien in Gods licht
als palmen opgericht.
Hun lot zal in zijn hand zijn.
Zij zullen vruchten dragen
voor 's Heren heiligdom
tot in hun ouderdom,
tot in hun grijze dagen.
Welsprekend is hun leven;
God is hun heil, hun rots!
Ik loof de daden Gods,
zijn recht is hoog verheven.

Uit de nieuwe berijming
van Psalm 92
door W. Barnard,
1967

.

Purpaleanie and other Permutations is organized by the age when a permutation took place. Sometimes event and permutation happen at the same time and classification is no problem; "Barnyard Miracle" is an example. Sometimes the permutation follows the experience by three decades or more; "Delayed Reaction" is an example. The time of permutation, not the time of the experience on which the permutation is based, is the organizing principle.

The Banner published most of these permutations. *Dialogue* first published "Purpaleanie"; *Voices* first published "Afternoon with Eliot." Permission has been secured from all editors for the pieces republished here.

The booklet would be impossible without the sponsorship and support of the Dutch Immigrant Society and without the willingness of Mr. Carl Vandermeulen and the Middleburg Press to take a risk.

All characters, including the "I," are fictitious. The attitudes and states of mind are accurate to my experience of life in Sioux County. If my presentation of Sioux County life offends anyone, I beg forgiveness. I hope that my own forgiveness for my past vexations with Sioux County is clear on every page. I write more to celebrate a vanishing style of life than to censure it—though the record of any life short of the New Jerusalem must contain censure.

Sietze Buning

Orange City, Iowa
Pentecost, 1978

Contents

Part I: Single Permutations

—In Childhood

—In Adolescence

—In Adulthood

Part II: Series of Permutations

Part I: Single Permutations in Childhood, Adolescence, and Adulthood

Permutations in Childhood

Shivaree

All ten of us
in the eight grades
of Holland Township Number Three
were going shivareeing after school
and no adult knew about it.

Angeline Vander Zwey
had not invited us to her wedding,
even though since before we could remember
she had played the piano for our singing on Friday
afternoons and even though she had promised to ask us.
She was getting married at home, and by the time she had invited
her relatives and Jake Wilting's relatives, the house was full.
We were too young to be invited to the square-skipping party at night
with our older brothers and sisters. "Sorry, kids," had been her only
preoccupied apology when she had played for us the last time a week ago.

Cornie, Henry John, and I in seventh grade and Rodney in eighth all hated
Jake Wilting as could be seen by the pictures of him in the margins
of our workbooks: his broad nose made broader, his male equip-
ment very small or very large but always evident, and his 4-F
leg as crooked as a chicken's. "Slacker" we called him
because he was not in the army, though no army
would have had him with his game leg.

Our teacher was as sexless as our mothers.
Ange had been our romance, her voice husky and dark
even on "Gracious Lord, Remember David," but best of all
on the war song: *From the factory to the mill/ from the valley
to the hill/ let's stand up and give America a thrill.* As her voice
sustained the note on *thrill*, her left hand thumped out a row of octaves
downward and her right hand upward. We boys hid the bulges in our overalls
under our songbooks. *On the farm, in the school/ let's have one golden rule:
Shout, wherever you may be:/ I am an American/ I am, every part of me.* The last
Friday on our way home in the horse cart, Cornie, Henry John, and I named
and described in detail which parts of Ange were American, every part
of her going to a slacker with a game leg and we not invited
to the wedding though earlier Ange had promised.

The next Friday
the wedding was at three just when we were singing. Our teacher could not thump
out the octaves. Her thin neck thinned even more for a high, pinched note
on *thrill*. We sang listlessly. In the farmhouse down the hill to the
north, Ange was getting married.
                                                        School over, we ran to the back
corner of the schoolyard where King, Henry John's horse, stood
grazing. Ten pairs of hands harnessed King and hitched him
to the cart. Seven of us into it. Cornie, Henry John
and I on the seat, the four girls on the floor behind
the seat, legs dangling out the back. Willis rode
a bicycle preceding, Gerald a bicycle following
and Rodney in eighth grade rode King
triumphantly in spite of the
awkwardness of sitting
on the harness.

On our way we handed out the noise makers we had stored under the seat:
a whistle,
some tin cans to bam, horse whips for the girls to snap on the road
from the back of the cart,
somebody's big brother's trumpet, a hubcap, and a tire tool.
We knew that real shivareers went
only in the dead of night to protest no invitation
to the square-skipping party. Anybody
too young to be invited at night was too young
to shivaree at night. Self-conscious as the only
afternoon shivareers ever, we turned into
the Vander Zwey drive. The ceremony was already over.
While refreshments were a-fixing
the company was singing some psalms. "Gracious Lord, Remember
David" they sang. Henry John
nudged us: "Hear her?" Ange's voice soared above everybody's: *Till*
he found a habitation/ fit
for Israel's mighty God, with the *found* high, prolonged, and dark, so that
the lump in my throat
could not be imagined away, even when the company started the second stanza:

Far away God's ark was resting./ It is with his people now. Rodney astride
King echoed "Now!"
We banged, tooted, snapped, and yelled. The psalm stopped abruptly.
Relatives appeared at windows,
wide-eyed at afternoon shivareers. In a minute Ange herself
was outside, white-gowned and carrying
her veil: "Hi kids, glad you came." She hugged Cornie
sitting on her side of the cart. She hugged
some of the girls. "Hey Mom," she called, "how about
some ice cream for hungry shivareers?" From the kitchen
doorway her mother called back, "Sure, but any
shivareers that get fed's got to sing first." "Well?" said Ange,
radiant and inviting. Henry John, chewing
a stalk of hay from the cart, asked whether Jake Wilting was in there.
Obviously he did not intend to sing
for the entertainment of Jake Wilting. Cornie's two little sisters cried.
Couldn't blame them; I in seventh
wanted to cry and they in third and fifth. Cornie had to quiet his sisters.
It was too much effort
for Rodney to get off King. The bicycle riders were out of breath, the others shy.
"You Sietze,"
said Ange. "You sing the war song. I'll play and help you."

So into the house,
past the Vander Zwey relatives
in the kitchen and the Wilting relatives
in the dining room to the piano in the living room.
Ange sat down at the piano, the veil hanging straight down
to her waist, the rest thrown in a heap in the seat of the rocker
in which she had been sitting next to Jake Wilting. Ange's cousins
peeked out of the bedroom. Ange and I struck up the war song. I do
not know why what happened next happened. Anger at Jake Wilting
with the game leg? (I could see it tucked under his rocker.)
Anger at Ange for marrying him? Or sorrow at losing
Ange forever? Whyever, it was not why Dominie
said it was: "Sietze is shy in a crowd."

Whyever it was,
when Ange sang the word *thrill*
dark and high and thumped the octaves
in contrary motion, I burst into tears as no
self-respecting shivareer has done before or since.
I hid my head in the white folds of her lap.
Ange's hands stroked my hair.

A moment later I   was sneaking out of the kitchen,
overhearing Dominie's diagnosis. My peers
were eating ice cream around the cart,
the waitresses serving them directly
from the crank freezer on the back
of the cart. I did not join them.
I dodged between cars, between
grove and chicken coop,
and to the road.
The horse cart
would be going right.
I went left. I chose to walk.
Everyone in the cart would know all
from the waitresses. At home I wrote
a letter: "Dear Ange, I love you. That is why
I cried. Sietze." I sealed it in an envelope and
addressed it to Mrs. Jake Wilting. I put a stamp on it.

On the way to the mailbox
I tore it all to bits.
I buried the bits
under a cowpie
in our pasture . . .

and have never seen Ange again.

Benign Neglect

Dad's Uncle Evert's eightieth birthday.
Who would remember if we forgot?
But we could not go see him—
not with the threshers here.
"Sietze, take your bike to town,
go to Hessel's bookstore,
buy any book in Dutch,
bring it to Uncle Evert in the old people's home—
he still loves to read—
and hurry back
because you need to tend the blower."

Only three Dutch books at Hessel's.
Eenie meenie minie moe.
Six minutes for Uncle Evert's eighty years
and nine miles home to tend the blower.

Rain the next day—no threshing—
and Uncle Evert sent the book back by mail
with a note. He appreciated the thoughtfulness,
but he found he had no compelling interest
in Wielenga's *Exposition of the Marriage Form*.
And did the book have anything to do with
the song Ed and Winnie had arranged
to be sung for him over the radio?
"Yield Not to Temptation"?

War and Peace

Coming to the house for breakfast after milking,
I asked, "What star is that in the southwest, Dad,
still so bright with the sun coming up?"
                                        "That's no star,
Sietze. It's moving and it's coming this way." In minutes
a floating contraption hovered above our farm. A machine growled
and ground out a leaflet which fluttered down to the ground,
but we had no time to read it. The contraption
was landing in our pasture.

You grabbed a scythe, I a pitchfork
and we ran to the pasture. Neal, Steven,
Cornie, and seven other neighbors from farther off—
all on their way to their houses for breakfast when we were,
milking finished—had seen the same apparition in the heavens.
Neal came on foot with a haying rope for tying up whatever needed
tying up. Neal's hobbling wife pursued him through the cornfield
calling plaintively: "Neal, Neal, are there any Germans in it?
Let me know if there are any Germans. I remember some German.
Don't kill them right away if they speak German." D-Day
one week past and we were all edgy. Had the Germans
elected to launch their counter offensive
in Sioux County and in our very pasture?

Steven, yelling "It's a sign of the times,"
galloped over at full tilt on his bay stallion
and brandished a twelve-guage shotgun none of us knew
he owned. Cornie came in his Model A and lifted an ax
and tire tool out of the trunk.
                                    Twelve of us stood in a ring
around the contraption, closing in for the kill. Whenever Steven
urged his stallion a step nearer without perishing, all of us took
a step nearer. Neal's wife caught up and continued her monologue: "Just
let me talk to the Germans." Suddenly the contraption growled and ground out
a leaflet.
            All of us sprang back.
                                    Steven's stallion retreated at full gallop.
How proud I was when you said, "Let's read the leaflet." Scythe in hand,
you walked to the contraption and picked up the paper. "Whoever finds
this leaflet, mail it to the Department of the Interior Weather
Service in Omaha. We are testing wind currents. Whoever
finds this weather balloon and machine, please deliver
both in person in return for an all-expenses-paid
trip to Omaha." Nobody cared to go to Omaha.
(Now if they had said Grand Rapids. Synod
was going on.) It was corn-cultivating
time, and nobody could go to Omaha.
Seeing it was our pasture,
everybody agreed it was
our responsibility
to get the machine
to Omaha.

The circle broke.
Neal took his wife's hand.
The two swished their shoes
through the long, dew-laden grass,
she a little disappointed that she still
had nobody to talk German with. Steven's stallion
broke into a gentle trot for home; the shotgun rested
upside down on Steven's shoulder. The blue exhaust from Cornie's
vanishing Model A mingled with the blue mist of just-past dawn. Swords
and spears had become axes and pitchforks again. After breakfast
you and I lifted the balloon and machine onto the grain wagon,
hitched up Frank and Snoodles, and took the whole contraption
to the depot. We put it on the platform. Unnoticed,
we didn't say a word to anybody. "Town people
made it," you said, "let town people
take care of it."

Leaving,
we heard it grind
out a last leaflet,
goodbye to us and hello
to somebody else.

Here's hoping
it got to where
it was supposed to.

Where the Tree Falleth, There Let It Lie

Mother
did not argue
about the faith.
How could she keep up
with you, Dad? But I knew
her to win one argument. Hardly
into our porkchops one evening, we got
a phone call that Abe, the Fuller-brush man
had blown his brains out with a twelve-guage shotgun
in his garage. We ignored our porkchops. Mother pleaded:

"I know we Protestants don't pray for the dead, but Abe is a
special case. Would you please?" You refused:
"Where the tree falleth, there let it lie."

"But just last week Abe was here with brushes—you were out—
and he said, 'Rena, you play some psalms and I'll sing,'
and he sang forty-two, sixty-eight, and eighty-four.
Knew them as well as you or I, mind you, and knew
some, like seventy-two, that I didn't even know.
He sang so hard, he forgot to ask me to pay
until I reminded him. How can such a man
be delivered up to Satan and despair?"
"Where the tree falleth, there let it lie."

"Then to comfort me pray for Abe. I feel responsible. I
played those psalms, sure, but I never said, 'Abe,
do you ever feel that your heart thirsts for God
like a deer for water?' I never said, 'Abe,
though you walk through trouble sore/God
will restore/ your fainting spirit.'
If only I had said it, Abe might
be alive now." "O Dad, do it," I whispered.
"Where the tree falleth, there let it lie."

"I know what you mean by 'Where the tree falleth there let it lie.'
You mean that Abe had no time to ask forgiveness for this last sin.
So, you think, Abe must be unforgiven. But if all Abe's sins—
past, present, and future—were forgiven on Calvary, would God
still flunk him for not crossing his *t*'s? That's work
righteousness. Nobody gets saved because of asking
or not asking, but because God is merciful—
though usually, I admit, people ask."
Her last qualifier cost her this one.
"Where the tree falleth, there let it lie."

"All right, Ben. Take forgiveness of sins once more. Past, present
and future sins are all forgiven for Christians on Calvary. Still,
it's no more than right for Christians to ask God to forgive each
new sin—a kind of courtesy-like, to tell God we appreciate
the forgiveness of the new sin—not that it wouldn't be
forgiven if we didn't ask it. If asking forgiveness
for sins already forgiven is proper, then praying
for Abe is also proper. We shouldn't take any
of God's mercies for granted." Did you waver?
"Where the tree falleth, there let it lie?"

"Ben,
Ben, Ben,
it's not only
Abe or me, but you!
Look at you! You haven't
eaten your porkchop either!
And as for 'Where the tree falleth
there let it lie,' moving a sawed-down
tree is impossible for a person single-handed,
but for God it's like rolling off a log." You changed
the quotation: "God's greatness is unsearchable."

You were not agreeing with Mother. Yet the unsearchableness
of God raised the debate above whether any Protestant
had ever done this before or what would the preacher
say if we told him. Encouraged, Mother used her
strongest argument: "Abe will go wherever God
has planned, but is it impossible that God
has also planned that Abe will join
the other saints again in answer
to our prayer? Then how can we
refuse to pray?" For the first
time your response was not a
quotation: "I suppose it isn't wrong to tell God we want Abe saved."
Do
you
remember
your only prayer
for the dead, Dad,
Protestant patriarch
that you are? "Be as gracious
to our friend Abe as your decrees
and righteousness will allow, and help
us all to enter in at the strait gate. Amen."

I
hope
that your
brief prayer
improved Abe's
accommodations amid
the bewildering corridors
of eternity, Dad. Neither you
nor he had travelled much. I know
that the tree which had fallen
on our hearts felt a little
lighter, moved,
                rolled
over, settled, moved
again. I could even
imagine the dead
weight being
gone some-
time.
Was it Mother, you, or God who worked that miracle?

Through tears, we even began to pick at our cold porkchops.

Permutations in Adolescence

Greasing the Windmill
June 11, 1944

It took Dad and me from afternoon on one day
until sundown the next
to grease the windmill.

The first afternoon we went to town
for a six-pack of beer,
put the beers into a gunny sack,
and hung the sack in the well on clothesline.
The mill above the well looked shorter than forty feet.

The next morning after milking and breakfast
we walked into the pasture.
Dad had an empty bucket to drain the old oil into
and I new oil in a new tin can.

Dad sighed
and started up the ladder,
each foot on a step for five steps,
then both feet on one step for three steps,
and then stood on the eighth step
complaining of dizziness.
He came back down.

It was my turn.
I made it twelve steps up,
one foot on a step but breathing hard,
when Dad called up that I had the new oil.
I had to go back for the empty bucket.

It was harder my second time
and slower with the bucket. The whole mill
shivered in sympathy. I managed only to peek
onto the platform, to lift the empty bucket above
my head with my free hand, and tip the bucket
onto the platform. Then I too was dizzy.
I came down, the old oil
still undrained.

Getting the better of ourselves
proved time-consuming. By now it was
coffee time. In the kitchen we admitted
to Mother that all we had achieved
was an empty bucket
on the platform.

Mother reminded us that my brother Klaas,
now, alas, in service,
used to grease the mill on his way to catch
the school bus,
starting out a half-hour early. And he never
even had a drop
of grease on him at school that day.

Mother reminded us that Gerrit Henry,
Klaas's friend around the corner,
not in service and available,
went up his dad's windmill
with the full can **and**
the empty can,
drained the old
oil, spread-eagled
himself flat against
the wheel, and had his dad
put the mill in gear. Afterwards
he said it had been better than a
ferris wheel. Running the mill
had got the last drop of oil
out, and he had added new oil
before coming down, all in one trip.
Why couldn't we be like that?
She might as well have said,
"Napoleon:
now there's a hero for you!"

In the pasture after coffee
Dad said, "We'll never make it
without the beer." He had hoped
he could bring the six-pack back to
Doc's Cafe, untouched. The trickle
and then the drip from the gunny sack,
the haul of the cold clothesline, and then
the beer itself, all would have restored us
if we had been thirsty and tired. We were
afraid, not thirsty and tired, and the
beer was our bitter anesthetic.
We needed a bottle apiece
for a full dose.

It was guilt
and not the beer
that got Dad to the top.
He had to prove to himself
that the beer had been necessary.
How explain the beer to God come Judgment
Day if he couldn't show that the beer had helped?
I cheered when he made it: *Oranje boven!* and I cheered
again when he opened the petcock and drained the old oil out
into the bucket I had delivered earlier at such pain. But his eyes
were bright as brimstone looking down, the guilt still there.
How could he ever know for sure he hadn't faked the fear
to justify the beer? He trembled all the way down,
step by step, rung by rung, the full bucket
tilting ominously as he changed it from
one hand to the other. The wind
whipped spatters over his bib-
overall and cast-off Sunday
tie. I remembered Klaas
greasing the mill,
clean.

We put the windmill in gear.
Three revolutions would have cleaned it
but we let it run longer to get it really clean.
Need I add that nobody was spread-eagled against the wheel?
We talked about the relativity of height, depth, space, and time,
postponing the minute when I would need to go up with new oil.
When we could think of no more to say, I started up.
On the twelfth step I glanced at my wristwatch.
We had talked for a half-hour; it was an hour
since our beers. "My beer's worn off,"
I called down, "I'm dizzy from the height.
I'm coming down for more beer."
But what would Mother say
if she smelled the beer
at dinner?
We decided
to wait till
afternoon.

At dinner Mother assumed
we were finished.
She greeted us like conquering heroes.
We had to admit only the old oil was drained out.
Had she known that, she muttered,
she would have made sandwiches
and not killed herself fixing porkchops
and apple pie, and
enough was enough,
we should get Gerrit Henry.

I waved her still
with bravado I didn't feel
and Dad prayed at table.
He might as well have prayed outright
for God's blessing on my perilous journey.
As it was, he prayed for God's blessing
in all difficult circumstances
and paused and swallowed.
No doubt from that moment legions
of angels hovered around me
but I was too frightened
to consider angels.
At prayer I considered
these fragile folded bones called
hands and at dinner I choked
on my porkchop and refused
my pie.

After dinner
the windmill had doubled in size
in the full glow of an Iowa afternoon.
Dad and I began with a beer apiece on the ground.
Who knows? If I failed again, he would need to be ready.
Actually, I surprised us both. I scrambled up, poured the oil in,
closed the petcock, and threw the empty tin down. It bounced higher than Dad's
head! What a height, to make a can bounce higher than Dad's head.
Promptly I was paralyzed.
"You done real good," Dad called, "come down."
"Wait till I get a notion," I said, and didn't budge.

"I'll go home for tea without you."
I could do nothing.
"You got a piece of pie coming."
I could do nothing.
"There still are two beers in the well."
I still could do nothing.
"Must we get Gerrit Henry to fetch you down?"
Mention of Gerrit Henry
made me go prone on the platform,
clutch the edge, hunt for the spokes
and undertake my quavering descent.

Then it was tea-time.
Mother poured us tea
but gave us no hero's welcome.

After tea, we did chores,
after chores, we milked,
after milking, we ate supper,
and after supper, Dad remembered the beers.
You couldn't return two beers out of a six-pack to Doc's Cafe.

That beer—
    with Dad in twilight
    at the mill
    all fear gone,
    well, as gone as fear ever gets—
that beer is the only beer I have ever enjoyed.

But Mother's diary is too spare for June 11, 1944:
"Dad and Sietze greased the mill today."
If ever I did a day's work, I did it that day.

Auld Lang Syne

The dominie had declined a call
to be the dominie of a big city church
and our church was having a surprise party
to thank him for staying.
           The Ben Vander Ploegs
invited him over with the Mrs. to be there no later
than 8:00. That was so that the dominie wouldn't have
other appointments and so he wouldn't be in his old clothes
and so his wife's hair would be fixed.
                   At 7:00 we began parking
our cars at the Reformed Church and walked the two blocks east
to our Christian Reformed Church through snow and wind. That
was so nobody at the parsonage looking west would see our cars
parked at our church.
           The church was packed
and we sat in December darkness
talking low.
           By 7:30 I was sitting at the organ
for at 7:45 Ben Vander Ploeg was going to the parsonage
to get the minister and his family and lead them into church.
When we heard the sanctuary door open, the president of the Young
People's Society would throw on the light switches, I would sound
a mighty chord, and the assembled congregation would leap up
singing, "Jehovah bless thee from above."
                   When Ben Vander Ploeg
left at 7:45, my fingers were already in position
over a G major chord.
           All talking stopped.
It had never been so quiet in church,
not even during prayers.

                                    Then,
the door creaked open,
the lights blazed,
the chord sounded,
and the congregation
leapt up singing, "Jehovah
bless thee from above/From
Zion in his boundless love."
Except, instead of the mighty
psalm, I heard laughter drowning
out the organ. It hadn't been the dominie
at all. The janitor, Albert Van Dongen
had just finished shoveling the dominie
a fresh path to the party, and so he was
arriving after the rest of us.
                        What began as the janitor's
triumphant entry changed into chaos. A hysterical lady
dabbed at her eyes, one man threw a hymnal into the air
and children yelled.
                    In the midst of this commotion
Ben Vander Ploeg arrived with the dominie and Mrs.,
and like the foolish virgins, we not ready.
I sounded the chord, but nobody heard it
for the racket.
                    When things settled down,
Dominie asked, "What is Sietze doing up front
at the organ?"
                    That set everybody off again.
Finally
Ben Vander Ploeg
got us quiet and
asked us to sing
"Auld Lang Syne"
without anybody
at the organ.

Strange Religion

Uncle Walter and Aunty Sue
sent a prayer request with their Christmas card.
Their Ardene was marrying a man of a strange religion
and moving across the state.

Next Christmas Sue and Walter
were across the state for Ardene's baby girl.
"Named it 'Phillipus'," some uncle reported.
"Or 'Philatelist'," some cousin spoofed.
"Poor baby," some aunty clucked.

Back with us, Walter and Sue
told about the strange religion:
"They bless their food before meals
but they never read the Bible afterwards
and on Sunday, Elmer washed the car before church."

Mother and Dad sent a dress for the baby
with a homemade card which read, "God's covenant bonds
will stand forever," though Dad reminded Mother
that all covenants contain two parts
and anybody who goes off marrying
riffraff breaks a chain
that could have gone on
for a thousand
generations
else.

Ardene's "thank you" mentioned she was a leader of Y-teens
("What's that?"),
her Christmas card the following year told how Elmer was skipping
lunch on Tuesdays and sending the money to a mission in Madagascar
("Sounds like work righteousness"),
and just before Christmas two years later she sent word
she herself had been ordained an elder—a lifelong term
("Keep our children, O God, from false prophets").

Hitchhiking home for Christmas my first year in college,
snowbound across the state,
I was at Ardene's house for a weekend.
Phyllis, her oldest daughter in junior high,
planned to be a missionary in Madagascar.
The younger children—one too young to talk—
sang "Precious Jewels."
Elmer was gone Friday evening getting the Christmas cantata ready
and all day Saturday bringing Christmas baskets to the poor.

At 9:00 each evening Elmer, Ardene, and Phyllis read the Bible
and knelt for prayer.

Ardene's strange religion:
Presbyterian.

Barnyard Miracle

Paulina
the heifer
would not stand
still while I milked
her. Five times she had
kicked
so viciously that the steel
hobbles had sprung from her
legs.
Despite the tender welts
where the hobble clamps
had been attached,
she was angry
enough
to do it
again.

The fifth
kick
had lost me
the milk so I
was angry too.
In childish temper
I took the gutter shovel
and beat Paulina
five,
eight
eleven
strokes
until I heard
your voice,
Mother.

You
were in
the barn
for heifer
milk for oyster
stew. Other milk
will do but heifer
milk is better. "O
Sietze, Sietze, God's
blessing can never rest
on such temper." You went
to the heifer's head, served
her an extra portion of corn
meal, and talked to her
woman-to-woman. "You
need to be quiet in-
side, Paulina, in
order to be quiet
outside." And
Paulina stood
perfectly
still . . .

still
too while
I finished
milking her.
And I wondered
what manner of wo-
man you were that even
the raging Paulina obeyed
you. And, what's more,
in addition to the
pailful spilled,
she still gave
enough for
oyster
stew.

First Lesson in Rhetoric

Father's
fellow elder
Marius called in-
frequently. Did his talk
leave too little or too much
to the imagination of the emerging
adolescent trying to sleep in the room
above with an open register between?

"Confession of guilt at consistory meeting is not enough.
Better to have them stand up at a service. Better to purge
the unclean thing from among us. There are more and more
shotgun weddings. Nothing to be afraid of, standing up
in church, not after sinners stand before God and confess.
Besides, it's a chance for the church to welcome back the
wayward. A truly Christian couple would prefer it."

Several such visits—the cases different
but the rhetoric identical—and *rhetoric*
not even part of our active vocabularies—

and then a visit from Marius with a new
rhetoric:

> "Our Martha
> loved unwisely.
> Our Martha must keep
> the baby. Our Martha
> so repentant, so sensitive.
>
> Must our Martha stand in church?
> Her mother will die—blood
> pressure over two-hundred
> right along. Our Martha
> loved too well. Our
> Martha . . . ."

Did the differences in rhetoric leave
too little or too much to the imagination
of the emerging adolescent, ear at
the register? And none
of us—not Marius,
not Father, not
I—even aware
of the word
rhetoric.

Permutations in Adulthood

Delayed Reaction
In Memory of HVG

"Today is review.
John,
What is your only comfort in life and death?"

"That wasn't in the catechism lesson this week."

"Ivan,
What do you mean by the Providence of God?"

"I can't remember."

"Willis,
What do you mean by *a holy catholic church*?"

"I don't know."

"Sietze,
What does God require in the third commandment?"

"I don't care."

"I don't care?
Did you say *I don't care*?
I have bowed until I can bow no more.
Nobody says *I don't care* in my class."

You grabbed your grubby Stetson.
You opened the door.
Pale and shaking, you yelled,
"I would rather have you say *God damn* than *I don't care.*"

We laughed,
surprised at the words you knew.

It didn't occur to me until now
that *God damn* and *I don't care*
mean the same thing.

I wish I could tell you
who must have cried "Woe is me" all the way home
what a good catechism lesson that was
on the third commandment.

The Valleys Stand So Thick With Corn

It was the year your dad had typhoid fever,
the second year we were married—Klaas was a baby—
and during corn-picking time. Well, really it was past
corn-picking time. Dad still wasn't better and he couldn't pick
but fifty bushels a day. He never was much for picking corn. O
he'd pick his hundred bushels in a day when he was well, but
each ear came out in five motions. You could see him think
to himself, grab ear with the left hand, hook husks
with the right, rip husks off top with left, throw
ear onto wagon with right, say giddap to horses.
With me it was more natural-like. My hook
ripped the leaves while I hollered giddap
and I was already on the next ear before
the last one hit the bangboard. It is
not ladylike, of course, to pick corn
and I only really ever sneaked some
picking when I brought Dad tea.
He'd have his tea and sandwich
and I'd pick two rows of corn,
right in my dress I'd do it.

But the year he had typhoid
Dad needed more help than at tea.
One morning while he was milking,
I got into one of his blue shirts
and one of his blue bib-overalls, only
I didn't put a tie on. One thing about
Dad, he never picked corn or milked a cow
without a cast-off Sunday tie on. I tied
a red hanky around my neck instead of a tie,
kinda pretty-like. But gracious, I was a sight
because when your dad came in from milking, he looked
at me like I was ready for the asylum. But I said, "Ben,
see here. I'm picking corn with you all day. Next week's
Thanksgiving and the corn not picked yet. What will the Vander
Ploegs say? I won't dare to go to church Thanksgiving Day." Well,
he sputtered that my place was in the home, especially now that he was
an elder and had to set an example. But, I arranged with your Aunty
Dena anyway to look after Klaas. When Ben had harnessed Frank and
Snoodles, he stopped in the driveway on his way to the field
which I took as invitation. We were in the field at seven.

By ten we had our first fifty-bushel load, what it took until
noon for Dad well and until night for Dad this year.
Those ears just hummed against that bangboard.
Three rows at a time we picked, Dad the one
next to the wagon, I two rows over,
and we both picked the row between us,
only I picked most of it. Your dad was weak.
Besides, he had to shovel the corn into the crib
whenever the load was full. Then I'd give Dena a hand
in the house, with Klaas and the cooking. Well, we were on our
third load—we had a goal of one-hundred-fifty bushels, three loads,
half again as much as Dad could pick, well, and three times as much as
Dad could pick these days, weak.

As I say, we were on our third load
when Dad looked up and said,
"I think there's a car waiting for us at the end." "It could be
pheasant hunters not looking for us,"
I said and kept on picking. Dad said, "It looks to me like a
Whippit." That hit me. There was only one:
Dominie Breen's. "Ben," I said, "I cannot disgrace you.
I will hide on the wagon." I climbed on the wagon
and covered myself with corn ears with barely
enough room to breathe. Partly I was hiding from Dominie
and partly from the ears Dad was throwing.
Not that they came so fast once Dad was picking three rows alone.
I thought we would never get to the end.
At last I heard their voices: "Hello, Ben." "Hello, Dominie." Hand-
shakes went on right in the cornfield.
Your dad insisted on it. It went along with wearing ties in the cornfield.
Then the chit-chat started: Mrs.
Kroon not making it much longer, the Krebs leaving the church—didn't agree
with Dominie that God loves
everybody, and the Visser boy still sick and no better and who knows what ailed
him. I've never seen your dad
so mealy-mouthed: "Ja, Dominie." "Really, Dominie?" "How terrible, Dominie."
"What I really came about," said Dominie, "is I need an organist on Thanksgiving.
Priscilla is gone to visit
kin in Minnesota, so could Rena do it?" Dominie was there to see me. Me!
"I could have stopped at the house
and seen her," Dominie continued, "but I saw your wagon here in the field
and thought it wouldn't hurt to bring up
the matter to you first, being both husband and elder." Yes, Ben
thought it would be all right. Rena
was out of sorts today. Better if Dominie wouldn't himself
ask her. Ben would let him know.
He was lying so hard he believed it himself.
Dominie was sorry to hear it,
hoped Rena would be better soon,
was sure she could do well
on Thanksgiving.

"And did the corn
get good and ripe this year?"
Dominie asked and stepped
onto the wagon wheel. "I remember
it froze-dried a year ago and
did not dry from ripeness. It was light.
But this feels better." The ear
he lifted off to feel was covering my hand
and he said later the whole mound
was wiggling. I can't remember whether I shook
from fright or laughter. *"Potverdikkie!"*
Dominie yelled in language neither Ben nor I knew he knew,
"You've got a warm body on your wagon."
So there we were, all exposed to God and each other.
I unladylike and not a proper elder's wife. Your dad not
a proper elder either, lying like that—I knew he told as many lies
as anybody, bless him, but Dominie didn't. And both of us knew Dominie
swore. So we all rode home on the wagon together. The Whippet stayed
in the field for now. Aunt Dena made us all tea, and how we laughed.
Before Dominie left, Ben suggested we sing something. Psalm 65
he wanted, the verse that goes "The valleys stand so thick
with corn that they laugh and sing." I used the hard
Worp accompaniment, not that easy De Vries,
and I didn't miss a note even though
I hadn't practiced. I laughed
at myself in bib-overall
pumping away at our
parlor organ.

On Thanksgiving
I was at the church organ,
the corn all picked and I in my best
velvet dress. I was thankful, I tell you.
I might have known it, and yet it was a surprise,
Dominie announced Psalm 65 for his first song. I pulled
out every stop, pumped like crazy, and made the organ go as loud
as it would go on the Worp accompaniment. I could see Ben in my mirror
singing hearty but sober, proud that Dominie had picked the same song he had.
Dominie was singing hearty too, and when we came to "The valleys stand
so thick with corn that they laugh and sing," he turned toward me
and winked. I saw him in my mirror. He winked! He did!
So seeing you asked, Sietze, I guess that was my
favorite time in church.

                      I had asked.
We had just come from Dad's funeral.
Mother had sung heartily
every stanza of every hymn, including
"The valleys stand so thick
with corn that they laugh and sing," sung
to the hard Worp accompaniment
not the easy De Vries. Mother had made that
arrangement herself on the telephone.
Annoyed and envious, both, I had said afterwards,
"Mother, you enjoy church. You even enjoyed
Dad's funeral." She agreed she had: "A bright spot
on a gloomy day." "What service out of your whole
lifetime did you enjoy most, Mother?" "That's easy—
the Thanksgiving service when the dominie winked at me
while I was playing the organ. Must have been fifty years
ago." "Why on earth did the dominie wink at you?"
"That's a long story. It was the year your
dad had typhoid fever . . . ."

Family Calendar

December, 1959: Dear children,
We are leaving the farm.
Dad has a new job
selling the *Des Moines Register.*

January, 1960: Dad is doing better
than the man before him
selling the *Des Moines Register.*

February, 1960: Dad won a maroon necktie
selling the *Des Moines Register.*

March, 1960: Dad won a fountain pen.

April, 1960: Dad won a briefcase.

May, 1960: Dad won a Bulova wristwatch
inscribed with his name
for selling the *Des Moines Register.*

June, 1960: Dad won an overnight trip
for both of us
to Des Moines.

July, 1960: Dad won a trip to the Minnesota
lakes for both of us. It will be even
better than Des Moines: fishing,
boating and resting.

August, 1960: Dad has a real hard contest coming.
The winner gets to go to Las Vegas.
Expenses paid by the *Des Moines Register.*

September, 1960: The contest is killing Dad.

October, 1960: Dad won the contest.
Next month we will both be going
to Las Vegas.

This is the last straw,
I say to my wife.
What will those innocents do in Las Vegas?
Why, we've never even been to Las Vegas.

November, 1960: As you can see from the postmark,
we are not in Las Vegas.
The *Des Moines Register*
had it planned
so we had to
travel on
Sunday.

Love,
Mother

52

Obedience

Were my parents right or wrong
not to mow the ripe oats that Sunday morning
with the rainstorm threatening?

I reminded them that the Sabbath was made for man
and of the ox fallen into the pit.
Without an oats crop, I argued,
the cattle would need to survive on town-bought oats
and then it wouldn't pay to keep them.
Isn't selling cattle at a loss like an ox in a pit?

My parents did not argue.
We went to church.
We sang the usual psalms louder than usual—
we, and the others whose harvests were at stake:

"Jerusalem, where blessing waits,
Our feet are standing in thy gates."

"God, be merciful to me;
On thy grace I rest my plea."

Dominie's spur-of-the-moment concession:
"He rides on the clouds, the wings of the storm;
The lightning and wind his missions perform."

Dominie made no concessions on sermon length:
"Five Good Reasons for Infant Baptism,"
though we heard little of it,

for more floods came and more winds blew and beat
upon that House than we had figured on, even,
more lightning and thunder
and hail the size of pullet eggs.
Falling branches snapped the electric wires.
We sang the closing psalm without the organ and in the dark:

"Ye seed from Abraham descended,
God's covenant love is never ended."

Afterward we rode by our oats field,
flattened.

"We still will mow it," Dad said.
"Ten bushels to the acre, maybe, what would have been fifty
if I had mowed right after milking
and if the whole family had shocked.
We could have had it weatherproof before the storm."

Later at dinner Dad said,
"God was testing us. I'm glad we went."
"Those psalms never gave me such a lift as this morning,"
Mother said, "I wouldn't have missed it."
And even I thought but did not say,
How guilty we would feel now if we had saved the harvest.
The one time Dad asked me why I live in a Black neighborhood,
I reminded him of that Sunday morning.
Immediately he understood.

Sometime around the turn of the century
my sons may well bring me an article in *The Banner*
written by a sociologist who argues,
"The integrated neighborhoods of thirty years ago,
in spite of good intentions,
impaired Black self-image and delayed Black independence."
Then I shall tell my sons about that Sunday morning.

And I shall ask my sons to forgive me
(who knows exactly what for?)
as they must ask their sons to forgive them
(who knows exactly what for?)
as I have long ago forgiven my father
(who knows exactly what for?)

Fathers often fail to pass on to sons
their harvest customs
for harvesting grain or real estate or anything.
No matter, so long as fathers pass on to sons
another more important pattern
defined as absolutely as muddlers like us can manage:
obedience.

Excommunication

With at least six other possible ways of handling it,
Benny Ploegster stood up, his suit still crumpled
from the night before, for his excommunication.
As soon as proceedings began three years before
(the consistory was not hasty), when his case
was announced to the church without his name,
he could have said,
                    "Churches are full of
Pharisees," and never gone to church
again, resigning his membership. Or
he could have said,
                    "This Carnes
church is full of Pharisees,"
and gone to a more permissive
church which does not ex-
communicate alcoholics.
He could have done so
even after his case
was announced
with his name
a year before.
Or
        he could have
moved away and made
a new start in a new
church. Or
            he could have
repented and given up alcohol,
though had any of us including the
overweight dominie, who pressed for
excommunication—"It sharpens up a church"—
comprehended what it is to give up a hand or an eye
for the Kingdom? Or
                    he could have continued going to church
but not have come on excommunication Sunday, though it would have
weakened his case: he only skipped for hangovers. Or
                                        he could have come
and not stood up.

But Benny—
motherless from birth
and now too old to marry
for who would have a drunkard?—
stood up. His father next to him
cried quietly.
            And why shouldn't Benny
stand up? One stands for Confession of
Faith, and excommunication is its reverse.
                         Why
shouldn't Benny stand up? He felt the full impact
of the bond written in ordinances against him: the rebukes
from the elders and the dominie, the promises before them and God
to reform, the patience of God and the church running out and the fear
of Hell.
           Why shouldn't Benny stand up? He knew that excommunication is a key
which seems to close but actually opens, threatening the sinner into grace.
How would it take, if he were not there to take it.
                         Why shouldn't Benny
stand up? To show that he accepted his alienation as his own responsibility when the dominie read the form? "Since by his stubbornness
Benny daily aggravates his transgression, he is to be accounted
as a Gentile and a publican. We exhort you to keep no company
with him to the end that he may be ashamed. He is excluded
from the fellowship of Christ and the church until he
amends his life."
                  Why shouldn't Benny stand up?
Jesus himself had set up the procedure,
followed by St. Paul, John Calvin,
and other fathers Benny respected.
Why shouldn't Benny stand up?
That in twenty centuries
there was not a single
precedent for bodily
presence of an ex-
communicant at his
excommunication
is insufficient
reason not to.
Each case is
private.

It was not in protest although the dominie thought so
and it was not in stupidity although the congregation thought so
that Benny stood up
for excommunication
and until he died of cirrhosis he attended as regularly as before.
He did not partake
of communion.
Like Jacob wrestling with God and saying, "I will not let you go until
you bless me," our Benny was wrestling with us and with God.
Though he lacked Jacob's talent for articulation, his standing
said as explicitly as its verbal equivalent:
I will not be cut off
as though I do not exist.
I am God's child,
all right,
God's naughty child,
but still God's child:
Benny.

And what of us who attended church regularly
out of custom and superstition
and without much desire
and without any
questioning
that we had
a right to
be there?
What of us
who had never
wrestled like Benny?
Though he did not intend it,
by standing up to be excommunicated,
was Benny excommunicating us?
                                        The church
is gone now, the lumber used for a cattle shed,
but in memory the place where Benny stood is forever
holy ground.

Was
Benny
excommunicating
me?

Senility?

The very dominie who baptized the baby who became me went senile.
We could tell because he refused to condemn sinners:
the deacon caught with our tithes in his pocket,
the farmer who attacked his hired hand,
the woman taken in adultery. All
he said of such situations, Seeds
of every sin lie in every heart.
All he would do, pray—for his
own sins too.
              Once when someone
asked how he was he said, O
Satan is bothering me so
today. Then we knew for
sure he was over
the edge.
            Is it
senility in me
that what we
called sen-
ility, I
now call
holiness
  ?

Diplomacy

Prayer
and fasting
went into the critique
as well as insomnia and loss
of appetite, not to mention the effort
of a carefully kept notebook.
                            Is it any wonder
Asa's voice quavered now that he confronted
the dominie face to face in the parsonage?

"On
June 5
in the morning
you said that immersion
shows what happens in baptism
every bit as well as sprinkling.
On June 12 you said in the evening
that God loves everybody. You were on
John-three-sixteen again. On June 19 you quoted
the Pope—about the need for peace. On June 26
you asked the Presbyterian minister to pray.
He used to be Reformed, but even the sister-
in-law he was visiting says he doesn't read
the Bible anymore—not after meals he does-
n't. And your Fourth-of-July sermon was
anti-American. When Jesus said 'My
Kingdom is not of this world,'
the founding fathers hadn't
even written the Constitu-
tion yet."

                    Asa
                folded away
            his notebook and afterwards
            he wondered how it had all happened
        so fast.
                        Any one of the charges was enough
        certainly to get the Consistory to reprimand Dominie
    and who knows? to get Classis to censure him or get Synod
    to silence him forever?
                        But the dominie had asked,
            "Is this your whole list, Asa?"
                                    "Ja, Dominie."
                "Well, Asa, those were certainly
                foolish things for me to
                preach. I'll try to
                be more careful.
                Bear with me.
                And now we
                    consider
                    the case
                    closed,
                    Asa."

    The case
    was closed
    because Dominie
    said so. Asa's in-
    somnia and loss of appetite
    disappeared because the case was closed.
    The prayer and fasting disappeared because
    the insominia and loss of appetite disappeared.
    And Asa sold his farm and studied to be a dominie
    because a dominie can call a case closed to avoid a fight
    and thus do a world of good.

Calvinist Farming

Our Calvinist fathers wore neckties with their bib-overalls
and straw hats, a touch of glory with their humility. They rode
their horse-drawn corn planters like chariots, planting the corn
in straight rows, each hill of three stalks three feet from each hill
around it, up and over the rises. A field-length wire with a metal knot
every three feet ran through the planter and clicked off three kernels
at each knot. Planted in rows east-west, the rows also ran north-
south for cross-cultivating. Each field was a checkerboard even
to the diagonals. No Calvinist followed the land's contours.

Contour farmers in surrounding counties
improvised their rows against the slope
of the land. There was no right way.
Before our fathers planted a field,
they knew where each hill of corn
would be. Be ye perfect, God said,
and the trouble with contour farmers
was that, no matter how hard they worked
at getting a perfect contour, they could
never know for sure it was perfect—and
they didn't even care. At best they
were Arminian, or Lutheran, or Catholic,
or at worst secular. Though they wore bib-
overalls, they wore no neckties, humility
without glory.
                 Contour fields resulted
from free will, nary a cornstalk predetermined. The God contour farmers
trusted, if any, was as capricious
as their cornfields. Calvinists knew
the distance between God and people was
even greater than the distance between people
and corn kernels. If we were corn kernels in God's
corn planter, would we want him to plant us at random?
Contour farmers were frivolous about the doctrine of election
simply by being contour farmers.
                 Contour farmers didn't control
weeds because they couldn't cross-cultivate. Weed control was laid
on farmers by God's curse. Contour farmers tried to escape God's curse.
Sooner or later you could tell it on their children: condoning weeds
they condoned movies and square-skipping. And they wasted land,
for planting around the rises, they left more place between
the rows than if they'd checked it. It was all indecent.

We could drive a horse cultivator—it was harder
with a tractor cultivator—through our checked rows
without uprooting any corn at all, but contour farmers
could never quite recapture the arbitrary angle, cultivating,
that they used, planting. They uprooted corn and killed it. All
of it was indecent and untidy.
                        We youngsters pointed out that the tops
of our rises were turning clay-brown, that bushels of black dirt
washed into creeks and ditches every time it rained, and that
in the non-Calvinist counties the tops of the rises were
black. We were told we were arguing by results, not
by principles. Why, God could replenish the black
dirt overnight. The tops of the rises were God's
business.
            Our business was to farm on Biblical principles.
Like, Let everything be done decently and in good order; that is
keep weeds down, plant every square inch, do not waste crops, and be tidy.
Contour farmers were unkingly because they were untidy. They could not be
prophetic, could not explain from the Bible how to farm. Being neither kings
nor prophets, they could not be proper priests; their humility lacked defi-
nition. They prayed for crops privately. Our whole county prayed
for crops the second Wednesday of every March.
                           God's cosmic planter
has planted thirty year's worth of people since then,
all checked and on the diagonal if we could see
as God sees. All third-generation Calvinists
now plant corn on the contour. They have the word
from the State College of Agriculture. And so the clay-
brown has stopped spreading farther down the rises
and life has not turned secular, but broken.
                       For
God still plants people on the predetermined check
even though Calvinists plant corn on the contour. God's
check doesn't mean a kernel in the Calvinist's cornfield.
There's no easy way to tell the difference between Calvinists
and non-Calvinists: now all plant on the contour; all tolerate
weeds; between rows, all waste space; all uproot corn, cultivating;
all consider erosion their own business, not God's; all wear
overalls without ties; all their children go to the same
movies and dances; the county's prayer meetings
in March are badly attended; and I am improvising
this poem on the contour, not checking it in rhyme.

Glad for the new freedom, I miss the old freedom of choice
between Calvinist and non-Calvinist farming. Only in religion
are Calvinist and non-Calvinist distinguishable now. When different
ideas of God produced different methods of farming, God mattered more.
Was the old freedom worth giving up for the new? Did stopping the old
erosion of earth start a new erosion of the spirit? Was stopping old
erosion worth the pain of the new brokenness? The old Calvinists
insisted that the only hope for unbrokenness between the ways
of God and the ways of farmers is God.

A priest, God wears
infinite humility; a king, he wears infinite glory. He is even
less influenced by his upward-mobile children's notions of what not
to wear with what than our Calvinist fathers were in neckties with bib-
overalls. Moreover, a prophet, he wears the infinite truth our Calvinist
fathers hankered after to vindicate themselves, not only their farming.
Just wait, some dark night God will ride over the rises on his chariot-
corn planter. It will be too dark to tell his crown from a straw hat,
too dark to tell his apocalyptic horses from our buckskin horses or
from unicorns. No matter, just so the wheels of that chariot-corn
planter, dropping fatness, churn up all those clay-brown rises
and turn them all black, just as the old Calvinists predicted.

Lord Jesus, come quickly.

Calvinist Sunday Dinner

(A Monologue in Two Voices)

Wasn't that a good sermon, Gertrude?
Orthodox. Such a rich Jesus
and such a poor sinner.
And what poor sinners
we all are, apart
from grace
of course.
> These potatoes are a little hard,
> Gertrude, too hard for the side of my fork.
> Hard to chew too. You say some rump-roast gravy's
> coming? I shouldn't really, for my weight, but it sure
> would help these hard potatoes.
Yes, what poor sinners we all are.
And how Dominie mashed up those Catholics.
Deprived of grace, they say they are. They admit
they need something more they haven't got—
> Pass the rolls
> and butter
> this way,
> Gertrude.
—but they won't admit they're *depraved*,
that what they've got is worth no more
than filthy rags. Do you remember
how he shouted? "Filthy rags!"
he shouted and hit the pulpit.
> The nicest thing
> about rump roast's
> the gravy, Gertrude.
Good talk for young Mrs. Vander Wey.
Haven't they been married two years come June?
Then it must be one year that dominie finished with her
on the Catechism. It keeps the Catholic nonsense reformed
out of her when Dominie hollers "filthy rags" the way he did.
It's like a refresher course in Reformed Doctrine.
> Great rump roast, Gertrude.
> The knife slides
> through it.

Yes, and when he got
to the cheap grace
of the Baptists.
"Cheap grace"
he'd sneer
to his
side.
        Only one-eighty per pound for choice
        rump roast, Gertrude? I can't believe it.
You value grace when you know you're totally depraved,
that you can't even find God if you wanted to, except you can't
even want to unless God makes you want to.
        Pass the green beans, Gertrude, please, with the vinegar.
It's all just that cheap come-to-Jesus stuff with the Baptists. O
they'll agree that they're desperately wicked—
        I need some more green beans, Gertrude, with vinegar and butter.
        I ate that first helping in two bites, they're so good.
—but we sinners can do everything for ourselves according to them.
We can come to Jesus, they say. We can stand firm in Jesus,
they say. And then comes the backsliding—
        Pass the meat and potatoes again, Gertrude.
        The diet's off. It's Sunday. We've just been richly
        fed in church and now we're being richly fed at home.
Backsliding.
That's what comes
of all that cheap grace.
And we've got a few in our own
church too. Baptists at heart and
backsliders. I see Johnny Poort sneak
to the tavern on Saturday nights, and others
see him too—it's reported at the elders' meeting.
        I'll clear, Gertrude, while you cut the apple pie.
On Sunday mornings he sits in church and cries. There's that cheap
grace for you.
        What about a little of that *a la mode* on the pie,
        Gertrude. I'll start dieting hard tomorrow.
Of course, Catholics and Baptists are duck soup
compared to the liberals. Liberals think
they don't need any grace at all.
        My, what good pie,
        Gertrude. Made
        from Spies,
        I'll bet.

Dominie knows how
to preach, doesn't he?
He turned all quiet and intellectual-
like about the liberals, did you notice?
He put it to them in that sincere way of his
that liberals are pompous and self-satisfied,
believing heaven is here on earth already.
The only way you can fault Dominie
is that he could have called
attention to the election
and reminded everybody
that liberals usually
vote Democratic.

Weeeeeeeeell,
let's close.
I'll read what the preacher
read in church. Best proof
text in the Bible for Total
Depravity:
> *Woe unto them that call evil good and good evil.*
> *That put darkness for light and light for darkness.*
> *That put bitter for sweet and sweet for bitter.*
> *Woe unto them that are wise in their own eyes.*

Our Father in Heaven
we thank thee for this pleasant Sunday,
for the delicious food and for the hands that prepared it,
for our orthodox church and for our orthodox dominie, and for his sound
sermon on Total Depravity. We thank thee that he has the gift of serving
it up so appetizing. We thank thee that it goes down so easy with us
and with the young folks too, most of them anyway. Bring many
Catholics, Baptists, and liberals to a saving knowledge,
and keep, if it be thy will, any more of our children
from marrying any more of theirs, for we know
unless they build on Total Depravity
they will never amount to a thing.
All this we ask with the remission of our manifold sins and transgressions etc

Why Freedom Wouldn't Ring

Christians from miles around came to the Van Roekel farm on the Fourth.
In the pasture a makeshift ball diamond—Middleburg against Carnes.
My big brother hit a home run for Middleburg with the bases loaded.
The after-applause hush demanded eloquence. He flicked the sweat
off his forehead and spoke in Dutch: "That's a right fine breeze
out of Van Roekel's slough!" Middleburg cheered again. Could
Patrick Henry have said it better?

> But Gerrit Rewarts,
> a poor neighbor
> of the Van Roekels,
> strode through the diamond,
> muttering, "These people
> call themselves
> Christians?"

On the speakers' stand, which fluttered in bunting,
the visiting professor compared Patrick Henry to William
the Silent, the dominie with the doctor's title spoke about
the rainbow as God's flag, and the piano tuner led the company
in "America" and "Wilhelmus," "Faith of Our Fathers" and "Open Your
Mouth and I Will Fill It, Saith the Lord," the Christian School principal
read a Dutch essay about Columbus, and Dad and three other farmers had a debate:
"Resolved: that there be a Christian Farm Bureau."

> In tatters
> Gerrit Rewarts
> stood at the fringes:
> "I've had me my fill
> of Christians."

After the ballgame and speeches the canteen opened with God's plenty:
choice of hamburgers or fried ham sandwiches, all donated by the butcher;
choice of cherrynut ice cream or butterbrickle, all donated by the creamery;
every mother brought her fanciest cake. The proceeds were for adding a third
year to the Christian High—how else would we revolutionize America? A dominie
fried hamburgers, the principal dipped ice cream, the teachers cut cake, and
the debaters counted change.

> Gerrit Rewarts looked on.
> He lived on a long, thin farm between
> railroad and highway. No tractor,
> no horse and cultivator even,
> could get into such a thin farm.
> His wife and he hoed it all by hand.
> They carried milk to the creamery
> in a chamber pail; the creamery
> paid them and poured it out.
> Their one baby had died;
> all they fed it was milk and eggs.
> They had quit going to church.
> They didn't have the right clothes.
> They weren't very bright.
> Only stupid people would live
> on such a narrow farm.
> He had no money for the canteen.
> "I'm sick of all youse Christians."

After the canteen, watermelon: free!
Watermelons had been chilling all day
in Van Roekel's stock tank. Fathers sliced
watermelons for their families on the feed bunk,
on fenders and running boards, on the tops of picnic
baskets,

> but I had no watermelon,
> no cake and ice cream.
> Gerrit Rewarts
> was following me:
> "Some Christian you are."

See, I knew the day before my brother would be playing ball
and Dad would be debating. What would my Fourth be?
As soon as we got to Van Roekels, I looked for two
chums: "Let's tip over Gerrit Rewarts' privy."
Somebody did it every year. Why not us
this time? I even had some soap
to write bad words on the
windows.
           But Gerrit Rewarts chased us away
           and now followed me,
           all afternoon.

Before we went home
the whole crowd gathered
once more at the speakers' stand.
Once more the visiting professor prayed
for our nation's future. Once more everybody
sang "America,"
           all but Gerrit Rewarts and me.
           Freedom simply would not ring for us.

Three decades later in a black ghetto
a dignified black pastor lectured me on a word
that interpreted my twelfth Fourth of July:
                        niggerdom.
           "All races and communities have it,"
           he said. "Most black folks are not
           niggers, most niggers are not black,
           and a true nigger never gets that way
           only by his own fault."
So Gerrit Rewarts' niggerdom
was not his own fault—not entirely—
but whose fault was my own niggerdom?
           On my twelfth
           Fourth of July
           I did not even care
           to go out at night
           to see the fireworks
           behind the Public School.

Part II:
Series of Permutations

A Series of Permutations
from Childhood
to Adolescence
to Adulthood

Purpaleanie

Purpaleanie

One

Eighteen and an uncle
I knew how you had treated me
at one, Dad, by how you were treating
the new grandchild.
                  Mother sang the ordinary
lullabies like "Hushaby Baby" to Jacquelyn at one,
but you sang your very own to the tune of "Precious Jewels,"
adding a beat here and there, not to make the words fit,
but to make the word fit:

Purpa -   leanie purpa - leanie   purpa -   leanie purpa - leanie

When Jackie cried
for the bottle being warmed
you sang words:

You will get your purpa - leanie. You will get your purpa - leanie.

Spontaneous
yet rehearsed
the way you had sung
to Klaas and me.

Two

At two
Klaas tells me
I hemorrhaged from behind
during corn-cultivating time.
Medicine from doctor was supposed to help
by evening, so you went cultivating,
though with the understanding
that if somebody waved with two towels
rather than
one,
the usual
come-home signal,
it would be an emergency.

Klaas,
then eleven,
remembers waving
with two towels.

You
came home,
unharnessed the horses,
got new medicine from town,
and sang me to sleep,
all before milking.

Klaas
does not
remember what,
but I know, because
once Jackie had colic
when you and mother were sitting
while I was home from college. You sang,

God will give you purpa leanie. God will give you purpa - leanie.

76

Three

At three
Jackie's
questions
were typical:
Why are Daddyandmommy
in Polyapolis? Why do potato
bugs have yellow stripes? Why
is your canary yellow? Why does
the baby calf jerk the milkpail?
Why do Frank and Snoodles roll over
and over?
          Jackie's questions were all
answered as mine must have been,
with genuine conviction
and in one word:
Purpaleanie.

Four

My earliest memory is of walking with you
in the pasture to pump water for the cows.
I stopped to examine a tan, brown, and bright
orange mushroom on a log.
          You said,
"That's purpaleanie!"
I
knew
by how
you said it
I had found
something special
but I was not to touch
or taste it. Not
now. Sometime
some other
mushroom
maybe.

The *sometime maybe* in your *purpaleanie*
was to break many a fall.

Five

I had only seen pictures of airplanes.
Once one that was lost
flew over our pasture
when you and I were
herding cows toward
the barn. They ran
away, frightened.
I was frightened
too, not that it
would hurt us,
but that we
wouldn't
live up
to the
event.
"May I
call to
it, Pa?"
"Go ahead."
So I called louder
than I knew I could:
"Purpaleanie!"
       When I had
proclaimed the sum of wisdom—
a fitting response to any visitor from
heaven—I was not frightened any more.

Six

"God hears me when I pray.
The pilot heard me when I called.
It made the pilot happy and it made God happy.
I helped the lost pilot find his way.
Purpaleanie is like heaven."

Thank you, Dad,
for never
contradicting me.

Seven

Still not sure
what purpaleanie
was I knew it
moved.
　　　　To the bedroom
with my mother when she dressed.
To any public bathroom that said **Ladies**.
And once
when you said
you liked the lacy
blouse my teacher wore,
didn't it move there too?

Eight

The geldings
had to wait until June
but early in May before any flies
we put a flynet on Babe the mare.

Three hundred
dangling strings
made Babe look like
what I now know is
a ballerina.

What did she look like
to you who had never seen a ballerina?

I
only
know
you called
my mother's
nightie a
flynet.

Nine

We
buying horses
at the sale barn
and passing behind
the long rows
of horses'
rears and
you with
a comment
on each horse:

"Too heavy for work."
"Jittery, he jerked as we walked by."
"Slow. Her head hangs too much."
"Too light. Can't pull."

And then
"This one,
of course,
will have a colt
soon."
  "But Dad,
that's a gelding."
"Aint that rotten?
Poor colt has no way
to get out."

Ten

You
thinning out
your herd regretfully.

You,
the customer, and I, walking
behind the cows, and you with a comment
on each cow.
          "This cow is the first in the barn.
Bossy." "This one has a bad left hind quarter, but
gets big calves." "This one gives sixteen quarts twice
a day." "This one gives milk yellow with butterfat."

And then
to your pet,
the blue roan,
the one you and I
pulled the calf from
with ropes when she couldn't
manage it alone.

"And this cow
is the best in the barn.
She doesn't give very much,
but she gives all she can."

Eleven

The blue roan in heat, you ill.
"Sietze, lead the blue roan to Vanden Bergs."
They and we traded the use of the bull for the use
of the end-gate seeder.
           I got our blue roan closeted
with the Vanden Berg bull and I sat outside the barn,
eaten with curiosity, but ashamed to disturb the blue roan's
privacy.
           Mrs. Vanden Berg came to the barn to wash the cream separator.
I volunteered to wash down the milkhouse.
                     Through the milkhouse door
through the long cow barn, the blue roan and the black angus bull
visible.
           I promised myself not to peek on the blue roan.
I concentrated on hosing.
                But Mrs. Vanden Berg,
the separator cleaned, stood in the doorway,
watching. Then I broke my
promise. I stood behind
Mrs. Vanden Berg, peeking
past her so she would
not see me looking.
I watched all of it
again and again
until Mrs. Vanden Berg,
bluff and hearty,
said, "She'll be
content after all that,
don't you think so too,
Sietze?"
         So she knew
I had been peeking.
I could not say more than
"Yes, thank you for the use
of your bull, Mrs. Vanden Berg,
and goodbye."
             And I could not
look the blue roan
in the face
on the way
home.

Twelve

Mother with erysipelas,
in and out of consciousness,
the left half of her face a running scab
and the winter the worst ever.

At school I fell behind
in biology and I wanted to cry
in lit reading aloud, "Whatever fades
but fading pleasure brings."

But you were a model
of efficiency in the barn.
And in the house too. Washing
daily with Aunty. Shoveling a daily
road for the doctor and minister. Getting
medicine and food from town daily. Daily
cooking. Writing to Klaas in the army
daily. Daily reading aloud to Mother
in a strong voice: "Let not your
heart be troubled," and "Birds
have nests and foxes holes
but the son of man has no
place to lay his head."

But one day, already dark, on my way to the house
after milking, I heard you cry out to Neal
the neighbor: "I can't live without her!"
You were sitting in Neal's car, parked
midway between house and barn,
and you cried again: "I can
not live without her!"
It was your house
and your barn,
but once Neal
drove away
O son of
man, you
had no
place
to lay
your head.

Not until miraculously Mother took a turn for the better.

Thirteen

"That poor boar.
Thirty sows to service.
One of these mornings he'll not be able
to get up. Then when he's weak he'll get
erysipelas or enteritis. If a boar can't get up,
don't call the vet, I say, call the rendering plant."

"Sietze,
when you've milked
the blue roan, don't empty
your bucket in the separator,
go feed it with all the cream in it
to the boar. Coax it down him, like it
or not. Even use the bottle and nipple if needs be."

And I
pouring half
of the blue roan's
golden milk into the trough
and filling and refilling a baby
bottle with the other half, poking
the nipple through the wall of the boar
pen and withdrawing the nipple abruptly
when he became too rough. And all of it
oddly sexless, a chore like feeding chickens.

Nor did it leap into meaning
when you said at table, "Mother,
coax another glass of milk down Sietze."

Not until you—
patriarchal in cast-off
Sunday tie with blue shirt
and bib-overalls—winked and grinned
at me behind her back while she served it.

Fourteen

It was something about how
the grocery clerk called you **Piers**
and not **Ben**
              and something about how
she complained about her husband, and about
how you said, "He's the best guy in the world,"
and about how she answered, "Yes, and I wouldn't give
a nickel for another just like him,"
                       and something about
how Mother snorted
when you reported it at dinner, though you didn't notice.
Or did you, behind your merry chortle?
                              There was something about it
made me think I never would have been at all
if you had found another place
O son of man
to lay your
head.

Fifteen

I on the single-row corn cultivator,
Frank and Snoodles harnessed in front
and nose-basketed to keep them from eating
themselves into a bloat on the tender corn plants,
knee-high already a week before the Fourth of July,
and you bringing me a sandwich and my afternoon tea.
What wild hair made Frank lay his neck on Snoodles
in an awkward embrace impeded by the harnesses?
What
made
Frank's
luddle
suddenly
hang
quite
low?
And
what
made
you
scold,
"Quit your horsing there,"
with a well-aimed clod at Frank's rear?

Why at the rear?
Why not at the luddle?
Or were you making a moral horse of him,
allowing him his free will, since a clod on the luddle,
and Frank would draw it up willy-nilly.
As a matter of fact,
Frank drew his luddle up
as promptly into his pouch
as if you had hit it head on.
Then, with a resigned shrug that jangled
the chains of the tugs against the cultivator,
he slowly lifted his neck off Snoodles.

Would you have thrown the clod
if both had not been geldings,
if Snoodles, say, had been a mare?
Was the clod
Romans 1
translated into Horse
in the service of God?

But what would you have done
if he had kept his neck on Snoodles' neck
and his luddle exposed? Thrown a clod at the luddle
next time? What else could you have done?
He nearly had the better of you!
Is that why you scolded
and threw the clod?
You knew how weak
the human grip
on horseflesh?
Or were you disappointed that,
while surgery had assured infertility
it had not completely subdued virility,
nor effected celibacy, the most desirable of all
according to St. Paul?

Was the clod
aimed at the horse
really intended for the vet?
Or for your own horseflesh?
Or mine? (You knew I had
an all-day date
on the Fourth.)
Or for the
complex-
ity of
sex?

There was a lot
I did not understand.
But you said to me, as though
everything was settled: "Look at him now.
As pious as at a Sunday School picnic.
Butter wouldn't melt in his mouth."

Butter from my dried-beef sandwich
was melting in my mouth, and even
then I understood one principle
so I can never forget it:

Horseflesh does not
expose its luddle
while in
harness.

Sixteen

Seven-fifty to spend for my girlfriend's birthday
in return for driving tractor during harvest.
Should it be a dangling bracelet or a jewelry
box? Agonizing decision an hour amaking
in the jewelry store.
          It turned out to be
the box: square, ceramic, yellow,
with three-dimensional purple
roses on the lid.
        No sooner
paid for than I wished it
to be the bracelet.
        But
in the car I showed
you, and knew
the box was
right.
    You
said only
one word
as—with
a naughty
grin—you
lifted the
flowers and
peeked inside:

PURPALEANIE!

Seventeen

Mother worried
that my sex education
was not complete, not knowing
you had undertaken it when I was one.

Mother called a family council
before I went to college.
Mother led off:

"Love is never sin.
    Lust is always sin.
Love is giving.
    Lust is getting.
Love always lasts.
    Lust never lasts.
Love is expressing yourself
    Lust is gratifying yourself."

And you, Dad,
suddenly agitated:
"This uncivilized English
language, with two words for the same thing,
only one is good and the other bad! In Dutch
lust means like wanting food when you're hungry!
Sure, it's getting,
               it never lasts,
                    and it's self-gratifying,
but it's not sin to enjoy food when you're hungry!"

Then you fell silent.
When you spoke again
You were calmer.

"When you get married, Sietze,
I hope it's for love,
but I hope it's for lust too."

Eighteen

My line at college bull-sessions:

"Puritans ruined
lust, just as bad poets ruined
love, just as psychologists ruined
desire, and just as doctors ruined
sex. Puritans all of them,
they took the fun
out of it.

We need
a new word,
any word, an arbitrary
word, a word made up special,
on the spur of the moment,
like, for instance,
purpaleanie."

My comrades
were scornful,
seeing only *purr,*
pal, lean, and *purple.*
I was scornful
of how dense
they were.

Now,
more than
eighteen years
after the scorn, I
see that I wanted them
to pick up at once
a word it took
you eighteen
years to
teach
me.

A Series of Permutations
from Adolescence to Adulthood

That Stone on Five Easters

That Stone on Five Easters: 1946, 1947, 1954, 1969, ????

(Commissioned for the *Paaszamenkomst* by The Dutch Immigrant Society, 1977)
(All characters are, of course, fictitious; the attitudes bear the accuracy. SB)

1946

My organ teacher,
organist in the American
Reformed Church in town, always played
"The Hallelujah Chorus" on Easter morning.
Immediately after it her congregation always sang
"Christ the Lord is Risen Today." What an opening!

At my own Christian Reformed Church
in the country we always had a Dutch service
on Easter morning. Before church our organist played
"Er ruist langs de wolken" and immediately after we sang
"De steen die door de tempelbouwers" from Psalm One-hundred-
eighteen.
              "When you get to be organist,"
my Americanized organ teacher said, "you've got to change
all that. You can't play 'The Hallelujah Chorus' and then sing
those dreary psalms right after. Your preacher is well-meaning,
just not quite with it about Easter music. When you're organist,
refuse to play unless they have an English service on Easter."

1947

The next year I was the organist.
After the afternoon service on Palm Sunday
I protested to the dominie. It would be proper,
I told him, to play "The Hallelujah Chorus" on Easter Morning
and after that to sing "Christ the Lord is Risen Today." Since
no Dutch version of "Risen Today" exists, there must be an English
service on Easter morning.
            I had not predicted
Dominie's response: " 'Christ the Lord is Risen Today'?
What kind of Sunday School song is that? It says right out
what Easter means without a shred of theology about Easter. Play
your Hallelujahs, fine, but the service will be in Dutch and begins
with *'De steen die door de tempelbouwers'*."
                        I reported
to my organ teacher on Holy Monday. I had not predicted
her response: "You Christian Reformed fanatics! Easter Sunday
and you sing an old-fashioned psalm about a stone! What stone?
The only stone in the Easter story is the stone in front of the grave.
Is that where Christian Reformed folks want to keep Jesus? In the grave
and you right with him, singing psalms from the Old Testament. And you may
tell your fanatic of a minister I said so."
                        I told him
on Holy Tuesday. I had not predicted his response: "Fanatics?
That woman calls us fanatics? All she knows is the music of two
centuries. Her 'Hallelujah' and 'Risen Today' are eighteenth century
and 'Low in the Grave He Lay' nineteenth. *'De steen die door de tempelbouwers'* is five centuries older than the first Easter, Jesus himself quoted
the psalm to predict his resurrection, Paul and Peter both identify the stone
of this psalm as Christ, the Old Testament Easter lesson in the medieval church
was this psalm, John Calvin started all festive services with this psalm
and all Dutch Easter services since the Reformation have begun with
'De steen die door de tempelbouwers.' So we're fanatics?
She is an ex-Calvinist who has given up her Calvinism
for provincial reasons."
                    On Holy Wednesday I told her. I had not predicted
her response: "An ex-Calvinist, he calls me. So I'm Reformed and not
Christian Reformed, but I know the Heidelberg Catechism as well
as he does, and he calls me an ex-Calvinist? You Christian
Reformed people all think you're God-on-wheels."

                               On Maundy Thursday
the Thursday of the New Commandment, I reported to Dominie.
I had not predicted his response: "She knows Reformed
Doctrine, but it has an English accent. Handel
wrote his 'Hallelujahs' for the English court.
'Risen Today' was written for the Anglican liturgy
and 'Grave He Lay' for the Methodist non-liturgy. Her theology
may be Reformed, but her music is typical English superficiality.
But that's how it is with people from the **Hervormde kerk**: bring them
to America and in a generation they are as American as Americans,
which in church music means as English as the English."
                                         All this I reported
to my organ teacher on Good Friday. For the last time, I had not
predicted her response; "He's calling me intolerant, *me,*
when he's the one who won't tolerate anything but psalms
nobody has heard of on Easter morning. If you ask me,
I say he's a pharisaical whited sepulchre."
On Holy Saturday I had a note from my organ teacher:
"Because of irreconcilable differences in our religions,
I suggest you discontinue studying organ with me. And tell
your pastor that as for him and his congregation, they can all
sit on tacks!"
                        On Easter morning I played *"Er ruist langs de wolken"*
and we sang *"De steen die door de tempelbouwers"* exactly
as we had the year before. When Dominie said afterwards,
"You could have played your 'Hallelujahs' anyway,
you know," I said in my most hurt tone,
"We wouldn't want to make it too
English all at once, would we."

Every Easter there were fewer singers
for *"De steen die door de tempelbouwers,"*
and by Easter, 1960, the church was gone,
the lumber used for cattle sheds. The song
and the kind of services that went with it
didn't take in the new land.
The dominie is dead.

My old organ teacher,
though alive, no longer plays.
In her church "The Hallelujah Chorus"
precedes "Christ the Lord is Risen Today"
on Easter morning, and nobody questions anymore
that God wants it that way and no other.

But majorities can be as provincial as minorities.
Each provinciality regards what is unlike itself provincial.

1954

I would finally have my chance to play
"Hallelujah" and "Risen Today" when I was organist
of the army chapel of the headquarters
of occupation in Tokyo.
The chapel would be full.
I would play "Hallelujah" just short of full organ.
I would play "Risen Today" on full organ,
choir and congregation singing.
Stars and Stripes had advertised the service.
The General of the Far East would be there
to read the Easter story.
The chapel would be packed.
All through Lent I anticipated Easter.

The only time in two years at the chapel,
it was full.
But when I brought up the organ for "Risen Today"
nobody sang.
Nobody sang except the choir.
Reporters and visitors had come to see the general.
Visitors found the song unfamiliar.
Regulars stayed away to make room for visitors.
Teenage children of officers were climbing Fuji.
Younger children were at an Easter-egg roll.
Officers' wives were cooking a breakfast for the General.
The visitors were too interested in the procession to sing:
the choir two-by-two, half-and-half men and women,
half-and-half American and Japanese.
Just behind the choir came the general
in full battle dress, with ribbons and epaulettes,
the Bible open to the Easter story on his upturned hands.
Behind him the Episcopal chaplain in his white vestment with red embroidery.
He was swinging the censer and the heady aroma of incense filled the house.
Nobody but the choir sang.
That couldn't be heard because the organ was too loud.
As the procession passed the organ, the chaplain whispered:
"Tone it down, for God's sake."
Easter, and I had to play more softly than other Sundays.

The general read the Easter story in a Texas accent.
The chaplain preached on American readjustment to a peacetime society
as evidence of the possibility of resurrections.
The congregation was bored once the general and chaplain had passed
in procession.
They remained out of courtesy.
Easter was most authentic in the communion
administered according to the Anglican Prayer Book.
All the familiar images of the faith were there:
"Behold the Lamb of God," "Holy, Holy, Holy,"
as the four-and-twenty elders sing it in the New Jerusalem,
the Nicene Creed sung by the choir in Latin:
"Credo unam sanctam catholicam et apostolicam ecclesiam."
All the familiar images were there except the stone.
That stone.
There was the papier mache stone
which the children made on Palm Sunday in the craft room.
After the Easter-egg roll, they came into the craft room
and their teachers assigned them by turns to hide in the closet,
others would roll the papier mache stone in front of the door,
and then the closeted impersonator of Jesus would leap out yelling,
"Surprise."
Or were they playing Easter Bunny?
Either way, there was the stone that gets rolled away
if only for the game.
But I missed the other stone at the head of the corner
and felt nostalgia for Middleburg as I've never felt it,
where a dwindling congregation would be singing
"De steen die door de tempelbouwers."

I had the daft thought
that the simplest way to teach this chapel-full about Easter
would be to enroll the lot in Dutch classes—
even the general's discontented-looking wife—
and then teach them to sing
"De steen die door de tempelbouwers"
and to understand why that ancient psalm
is so appropriate for Easter.

1969

By the time I got back to Middleburg,
the church had disbanded. Easter customs
in the other churches had all gone slick.
I looked forward to Easter, 1969,
because I was in Amsterdam.
Surely, there the Easter
hymn would be
"De steen die door de tempelbouwers."
The opening hymn was *"Christus
onze Heer verrees,"* "Christ
the Lord is Risen Today"
translated into Dutch.

> *Op de tweede Paasdag zat ik met mijn dominee
> een borreltje te drinken in de Bodega Pels
> op het Leidseplein. Ik had hem uitge-
> nodigd om hem mijn teleurstelling
> bekend te maken: een Paasdienst
> zonder "De steen die door de tempel-
> bouwers" is toch niet een Paasdienst op
> Gereformeerde grondslag.*
>   *"Maar," zei de dominee,
> "geen sterveling zingt nog Psalm 118 op Pasen.
> Al voor de oorlog was iedereen zo dik zat
> van die Psalm als een Paaslied, dat
> als het gezongen werd op Pasen
> zou het wel in Zeeland in
> klederdracht moeten wezen.
> Pasen eist een nieuw gezang,
> en als je een lied zingt waar je zat van bent,
> dan is zo'n gezang je een steen om de hals.
> 'Christus onze Heer verrees' is wel eenvoudig,
> en niet bijzonder theologisch, maar voor
> Nederlandse oren is dat juist fris.
> En waarom wou jij gisteren
> zoo graag zingen van
> 'De steen die door de tempelbouwers'?
> Om je ouders nog eens te gedenken?
> Je houdt van iets aparts?
> Is het sentimentaliteit van jou
> of beginsel, dit gezeur over
> 'De steen die door de tempelbouwers.' "*

En hoe kon ik zeggen,
"Het is beginsel met mij."
Zij hadden de dominee's rechter oog
uitgeschoten toen hij ondergedoken was.
Zijn rechter wang had nerveuze trekkingen
overgebleven van een diepe wond. Zijn vrouw
was wanhopig geworden toen haar man in het bajes zat.
Zij was aan de drank verslaaft geraakt. En hoe kon ik zeggen,
"Het is beginsel met mij om op Pasen te willen zingen
'De steen die door de tempelbouwers.'"
"Nou" zei de domine, "persoonlijk houd ik wel van
'De steen die door de tempelbouwers,' hoor."

? ? ? ?

The ultimate Easter song,
"The Song of Moses and the Lamb,"
is the most cosmopolitan song of all—
sung by every tribe and kindred,
every language and dialect,
yea, by every idiolect.

The ultimate Easter song
will sound to my Iowa dominie
like "Christ the Lord is Risen Today"
and to my Iowa organ teacher like the psalm
"De steen die door de tempelbouwers."
How amazing to find the ultimate
Easter song the very one
that each so loathed.

The ultimate Easter song
will sound like both "Risen Today"
and *"De steen"* to my Amsterdam dominie.
Suffering has made him flexible;
flexibility has made him
cosmopolitan.

The ultimate Easter song
will be as boring to that Army congregation
as the Easter music at the Tokyo Chapel Center,
unless an angel rolls the stone of indifference away.
The indifferent will not feel at home in heaven.

Will we?

Will I?

Four Series of Permutations
in Adulthood
Afternoon with Eliot
Long-distance Compliments
That Godless Babylon
Last Visit in Three Voices

Afternoon with Eliot
24 June 1976

I.

I should like the T.S. Eliot
of "Prufrock" to know that I did too
consider the intimate games as advertised
by pendulous breasts on posters outside Victoria
Station, but decided on an intimate game
of my own, finding the church where he
had been church warden.
Two o'clock.

II.

I should like the T.S. Eliot
of "Tradition and the Individual Talent"
to know I had forgotten which church it was.
The bookstore no longer stocked the biography
which tells, and the bookseller associated *Eliot*
with St. Michael's, which turned out to be locked.
Only the butcher of the neighborhood merchants knew
that the vicar lived at 4 St. Michael's Square. He also
knew that Matthew Arnold had lived at 2 St. Michael's Square.
He knew because his own name was Arnold: "No relation, governor,
but our shop's been here more than a century just the same. Matthew
Arnold got his meat from my great-grandfather, sir." The vicarage
was a sandstone townhouse identical to Arnold's (to Matthew's,
that is). The window sills were three feet thick. The vicar
recalled another vicar of St. Michael's named Eliot, a radio
padre of the '30's, calling Western Civilization back to
God. But check the biographies on the other Eliot,
was his priestly advice. He had a sermon to get
for the Feast of St. John the Baptist at five.
He directed me to the library on Buckingham
Palace Road at half-past three. On my way
I pondered two Arnolds, two Eliots, one
St. Michael, one St. John the Baptist,
one great tradition, and two
individual talents: his,
of course, and such
as it is,
mine.

III.

I should like the T.S. Eliot
of *The Wasteland* to know the library
had the biography with the information:
St. Stephen's, Gloucester Road. The biography
was on microfilm.
                        Back to Victoria Station on foot
and on the tube for 20 p. At Gloucester Station I met
my only former student in movies, buried in a newspaper.
I cried, "My favorite moviemaker!" Did he only look like my
student? Either way, his answer was paradoxical: "Drop dead!"

Did T.S. Eliot of St. Louis think of Ezra Pound as I did
at the sight of the Montana Hotel on Gloucester Road?
Did Missouri seem as far away to Eliot as Iowa
to me at the sight of the Montana?
I ate a Granny Smith apple,
shoring up these fragments
against my ruins.

IV.
I should like the T.S. Eliot
of *The Rock* to know that the small rock
garden was well tended, abloom with moss roses
and clematis, that incense lingered from the morning
mass for the Feast of St. John the Baptist, that the organist
practising Bach and Purcell was competent, and that the verger
remembered the seat behind the pillar which Mr. Eliot used,
not the seat prescribed for church wardens.

V.
I should like the T.S. Eliot
of *Ash Wednesday* to know that Valerie
had, according to the verger, been at mass.
Sole survivor, she represented Eliot's women
at the Feast of St. John the Baptist: Charlotte,
Annie, Emily, Vivienne, and Valerie. The verger's
eyes wondered about the American who asked what color
she had worn.
          "The blue trenchcoat she usually wears.
She rather favors blue."
                   "Blue of Mary's color,"
I wanted to say and said nothing, but now
I say: "Grace to the Lady for the Garden
where all love ends. Teach us to care
and not to care. Teach us to sit
        still."

VI.

I should like the T.S. Eliot
of "Little Gidding" to know
that for me, a Calvinist, St. Stephen's,
St. Michael's, Little Gidding, Calvin
Church, and the Gloucester Road Station
are all equally sacred and equally
secular. (Yet why had I come?) Prayers
for the dead are pointless;
where the tree falleth, there let it lie.
(Yet I found myself kneeling where prayer
had been valid.)

Kneeling,
I remembered
all I could about
saints and I faked
a little: St. Michael
the church warden of church
wardens, at whose church an evensong would begin in a half-hour in honor
of St. John the Baptist, his head grown slightly
bald brought in upon a platter, still asking, Art
thou the Christ or look we for another
St. John, this one my own, from
St. Peter's in Geneva, like
St. Peter's in Rome, where
Eliot the tourist knelt
as I the tourist was
kneeling at St. Ste-
phen's (for the
first Christ-
ian to know
martyrdom
is the de-
sign of
God)

in London Rome Geneva St. Louis
Unreal City for which St. Louis
embraced the idea of a Christian
society.

It was, you may say,
satisfactory.

Ten to five.

VII.

I should like the T.S. Eliot
of *Murder in the Cathedral*
to know I knew before
I got there from the
biography, the me-
morial tablet
would ask me
for charity
to pray for
the repose
of the
soul of
T.S. Eliot.
I knew and did not
know I had come to light
my first votive candle ever
for 20p, the price of one-way
fare from Victoria Station near
St. Michael's, where an evensong
for St. John the Baptist was right
now beginning, five exactly. I would
meet you upon this honestly: Angry murder
would be more understandable, so more forgivable
to my Calvinist elders than this 20p, than this votive
candle for T.S. Eliot.

VIII.
I should like the T.S. Eliot
of "Mr. Eliot's Sunday Morning Service"
to know that, before mine, only one candle
burned at his memorial
"invisible and dim."

IX.

And I should like the T.S. Eliot
of *Old Possum's Book of Practical Cats* to laugh,
because the naming of God is a difficult matter./ It isn't
just one of your holiday games. I should like T.S. Eliot to laugh
at the intimate game which lit the second candle beside his
memorial: for St. Michael, for St. Stephen, for St.
Louis, for St. Peter, for St. Mary, and for
the saint T.S. Eliot despaired
of resembling, who said,
"Christ must increase,
I must decrease,"
until he turned
an invisible
Christian
poet, the
John the
Baptist
T.S.
Eliot
was
meant
to be
and
was.

Long-distance Compliments
(from father to son)

I.
Ja, is it really worth it
that we make the trip
for commencement?
Couldn't you just as well
graduate by yourself
and then we will celebrate
when you get home?

II.
Sorry we couldn't be there today
for your wedding.
Why didn't you get married closer by?
Congratulations anyway.
And take good care of her, Sietze,
but don't forget
she can do that pretty well for herself too.

III.
Sietze, you mean it?
You read the sermon today?
And you only a deacon yet, Sietze.
I'm prouder of you now than when you got
married and when you graduated. I'm as proud
as my father was of me when I read my first sermon.
But Sietze,
did you remember
to change your voice
for the prayer? Sietze?
Sietze, are you there?
Sietze!

IV.
Congratulations, Sietze, on your doctor's title.
What is your book called again?
Say it slow so Mother can write it down.
A Linguistic Analysis of Words Referring to Monsters—
In what was that again?
How do you spell it?
B-E-O-W-U-L-F.
—*In Beowulf.*
Could you please send two-three copies?
So many people want to read it,
like Aunt Alice and Aunt Lyda and Aunt Gertie
and Art and Rodney
and Dominie and all the highschool teachers
and, of course, we too.
Could you maybe send four-five?

V.
Ja, is it really worth it
that we make the trip
for your university commencement?
We didn't go to your college commencement either?
Couldn't you just as well graduate
with your own family there
and then next month we will come
and celebrate.

VI.
You took the job at Calvin College?
Congratulations!
You'll be teaching our own Covenant children.
I know you always say you can do the Lord's work
just as well at Florida State or Western Arkansas,
helping Presbyterians be better Presbyterians,
Lutherans better Lutherans, and Catholics better Catholics.
But you've got to admit
you're always more sure of your own kind though.

VII.
Congratulations on the baby, Sietze.
Thanks for giving him my name.
Don't forget the main reason
any Christian couple gets a baby:
that the number of the saints
may be full.

VIII.
You have a Fulbright?
And your whole family
will be in Amsterdam
for a whole year?
O O O poor you!
Amsterdam
is such a worldly city.

IX.
Sietze, Klaas got elected and I got elected,
and we were wondering did you get elected?
Congratulations!
All three of us are elders
in different churches and different classes.
Sietze, see whether you can get sent to Synod
because if all three of us got sent
maybe they'd put our pictures
in *The Banner.*

That Godless Babylon

I. "Offense"

For Grandfather
one of fifty in Middleburg, Iowa
Orange City was that godless Babylon.

For you, Dad,
one of two thousand in Orange City
Sioux City was that godless Babylon.

For me
one of a hundred fifty thousand in Grand Rapids
New York was that godless Babylon.

Until I went there.
Dad, I refuse to see New York as the pattern for the New Jerusalem.
And I refuse to see Tokyo, because it is larger, as that godless Babylon.

It took me all this while to find out
that we in Middleburg are as good as they are,
Dad, in the godless Babylon.

No offense meant or taken?
Present company included though!
You pay your money and you take your chance, Dad?
All right then:

Grandfather's Middleburg
is that godless Babylon.

II. "Forgiveness"

You know as well as I, Dad,
what fun it is to laugh
at city people who forget
to turn off their sprinklers
when it rains and who eat dinner
after decent folks are in bed
in the godless Babylon.

You also know, Dad,
that God's forgiveness
is necessary
for all the godless Babylons.

It may be news to you
and Middleburg
that human forgiveness
is also necessary
for the godless Babylon.

If you had laughed in full face
of the absent-minded gardeners and late diners
your laughter would have been forgiveness
for the godless Babylon.

That is why I am laughing
in your face and Middleburg's,
forgiveness not only for what you have done wrong,
but for what you are:
the godless Babylon.

III. "Gratitude"

Forgiving any godless Babylon
Middleburg too
I find with gratitude
a touch of the New Jerusalem
in the godless Babylon.

Last Visit in Three Voices

(The three voices: "Father," 'Mother,' and Sietze)

I.

"That was you then
walking up the hospital sidewalk
in an ice-cream suit."

It had been,
in a lightweight gray-and-white
striped jacket
with blue bowtie and black slacks.

"Did you have to come
in an ice-cream suit?"

II.

"I wish you had come before.
Three weeks in the hospital without a letter.
I know you've been living in England,
but not a word.
I've needed you so."

"O yes, the cards you sent.
Well, to tell you the truth,
I cared very little for the cards."

III.

"Six people have come to pray so far
and all of them prayed good prayers.

    Except that the new minister doesn't use
    thee, thou, and **behoove.**

    The old minister only stopped between Ohio
    and California on his vacation
    and didn't pick up how serious it was.

    Uncle George got so upset he couldn't make it to *Amen.*
    I had to finish it myself.

    The Baptist minister knelt at my bedside—
    pointless, of course.
    God looks on the heart.

    Your brother prayed a beautiful prayer.
    I was so proud.
    You boys don't know suffering,
    but it's good practice for being elders.

    Simon Jansen—
        You remember our old neighbor from the farm?
        We used to thresh together, remember ?
        My father taught him his catechism.
        I prayed with Simon when his Richard died.
    Well, Simon prayed the best of all.
    He'd give many preachers a run for their money.

Sietze, you and I will pray tomorrow.
That will make it seven."

IV.

"I haven't eaten for two weeks.
It's going toward the end.
I'm sure I won't need the car again.
You sold your car before you went to England.
Bring the papers tomorrow.
You can have my car.
Good night, Sietze.''

"Good morning, Sietze.
I just put away my first breakfast
in three months. I slept better
than I have in weeks. It is great
having you home. You brought the papers
for the car? But Sietze,
I'll need that car again.
How else can I go fishing?''

V.

"Sietze, the food is terrible.
I crave rusk with cheese
        but fuss, fuss, fuss
        they float rusk on the onion soup
        and melt cheese on the potatoes.
Fuss, fuss, fuss
        they cut tomatoes into wedges for salad.
        I like plain coleslaw without tomatoes.
        I like tomatoes sliced on bread with sugar.
They never serve watermelon, even in July.
        They can't fuss over that.
They serve me cold milk at bedtime
        when anybody knows only hot milk
        with sage and cinnamon
        puts anybody to sleep.
        Salimelk your mother calls it
        learned from her mother.
        Mother even wrote down
        exactly how to make it
        and you know what they said?
They said it was too much fuss!''

VI.

"The older I get, Sietze,
the more I see we are pilgrims
and strangers, Sietze, on our way
to an abiding city."
           "The older I get,
Sietze, the more I long for a heavenly
city whose builder is God, Sietze,
is God, is God!"
           "The older I get,
Sietze, the more I want to
make a good job of it
for God. Like,
today is the fifteenth.
IPS sends dividends and tomorrow
Channing. Deposit them for me tomorrow,
Sietze, and make a good job of it."

VII.

"We have never in our lives sung so loud
as at the mission fest this year.
The music teacher stood up front
waving his arms and simply would not be satisfied
unless each song was louder than the last."

"Not that missions matter that much
to the music teacher, or that louder
makes any difference to God, to us, or
to the heathen. But isn't it funny
he could make us sing louder than ever?"

"If I get better
I sing no louder at mission fests
than I do on Sundays."

VIII.

'Your dad
is coming home
tomorrow, doctor
told me. This is the
last time he is coming home.
Five times in and out of the hospital
in one year, each time a little weaker.
Next time he goes he will stay. You get it?
Your dad is coming home for the last time tomorrow.
Sietze, I want to look my prettiest. I'll get on the phone
to the hairdresser right now. I'll buy the lavender dress
Starrets have in the window. I'll get new earrings to go
with it. We need rusks, cheese, tomatoes,
cabbage, sage leaves, and watermelon
from the store. Deposit his money.
Put the deposit slip on his desk.
Before we do that, you wash
the car for tomorrow.
I'll get the house
picked up. Before
we do anything,
you call Dad in
the hospital.
Say we're too
busy to visit
him today.
Hurry!'

IX.

'Hello?
O it's you,
Agnes. Such
an early call.
But if you had
waited, we would
have been gone. We
are picking up Ben in
an hour. You had heard?
Yes, he's much better, seemed
to pick up when Sietze came home.'

'Well, we really don't know how long
Sietze is staying. Over the weekend for
sure. But Irene and the boys are in England.
And he has very important work to do there.'
                                              'Yes,
I know it's only a month before his sabbatical is over.
Yes, they all have to come to this country in a month. Yes,
Irene and the boys can make the trip without him. Yes, it's good
for Ben to have Sietze here. But Agnes, Sietze has only one month left
for his work.'
                'What work is it? Well, he works with a very important man.
The man writes plays and Sietze writes books about the plays. Nobody
seems to understand the plays unless Sietze writes books about them.'

'Agnes, that has me stumped. I'll write it down and ask Sietze.
How did the writer get to be so important if nobody can understand his plays without Sietze's books when Sietze hasn't
even written his books yet?'
                            'Actually, Agnes, I don't
know a bloomin' thing about Sietze's work. I only
know it's very important. So important, I don't
even want him here with such important work
there.'
        'Yes, of course, Ben will get sick
again when Sietze goes. But Agnes,
Sietze is going and that's that.
Call up next week when Sietze
is gone and we're lonesome.
Thanks for calling.
Goodbye.'

121

X.

We
brought
Dad home
where he lived
on coleslaw, cheese
on rusk, and *salimelk*,
where he slept fitfully
by day and fretted
sleepily
at night. We all knew the end
was coming. You and he knew it was coming
just when it was supposed to, but you said nothing
like
 'Amen,
   Father,
     on
      your
       planning.'
        You and he knew
that nobody fails to fail in the end. You and he knew
no Sietze could give what you needed. You and he knew
God loved you both.
     It was enough
so you could let me go.

But you said nothing
like
 'Amen,
   for
   you'll
    see
     us
      through.'

You were to say, 'You musn't cry, silly,' at the funeral. You
were to say, 'What a surprise that must have been, gasping
for air one minute and singing **Hallelujah** the next.' You
were to say, 'Life is going to be easier now in some
ways. Lonelier, too. I need a nice teacher to
cook for.' But you said nothing like
        'Amen,
       when
      the
     cross
    weighs
   heavy,'
not for another half
year. Then you
who had
never
set down
two consecutive
lines, the very night
before your fatal
surgery were
to write
your
only
poem,
but you
can't kid
me who write
poems. You had
been working on it
without our knowing it
and maybe without your knowing it
either, through six months of widowhood,
through two years of Dad's invalidism, through
three-quarters of a century. It is the poem of a lifetime,
a real humdinger.
     Like a particularly sweet watermelon, like the new
lavender dress,
    like any preacher you liked:
         'Amen, Father, on your planning.
         Amen, for you'll see us through.
         Amen, when the cross weighs heavy.
         Amen, everything you do.'